CLAIRE

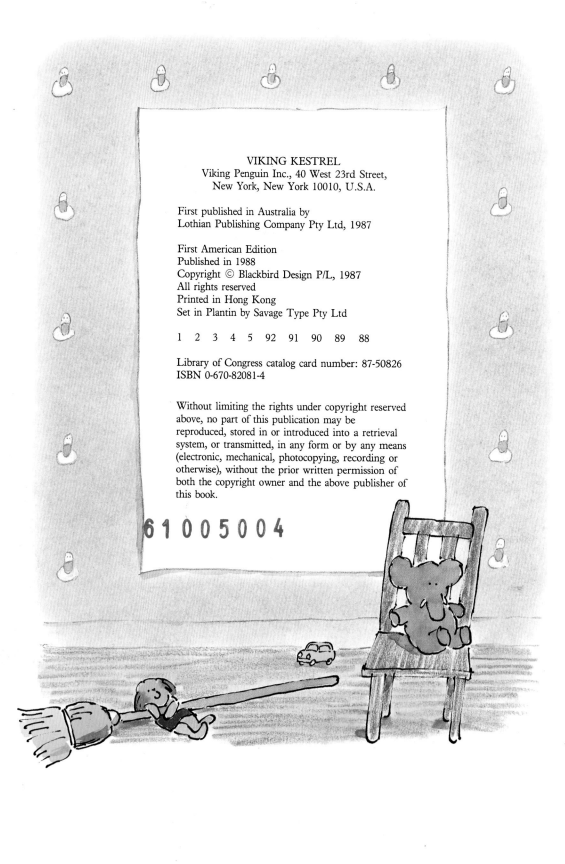

VIKING KESTREL
Viking Penguin Inc., 40 West 23rd Street,
New York, New York 10010, U.S.A.

First published in Australia by
Lothian Publishing Company Pty Ltd, 1987

First American Edition
Published in 1988
Copyright © Blackbird Design P/L, 1987
All rights reserved
Printed in Hong Kong
Set in Plantin by Savage Type Pty Ltd

1   2   3   4   5   92   91   90   89   88

Library of Congress catalog card number: 87-50826
ISBN 0-670-82081-4

61005004

FO

CRUSHER is COMING!

BOB GRAHAM

Viking Kestrel

Peter has just cleaned out his room.
He is giving all his stuffed animals
to his sister Claire,

because tough Crusher is coming
home after school tomorrow.

"Goodbye, Peter, give me a kiss," says his mom.

"Please don't kiss me this afternoon when
Crusher comes home, Mom . . ."

". . . and keep Claire out of my room when he's here, *please*."

"Crusher has come straight from
football practice this afternoon.
This is my mom . . ."

". . . and my sister, Claire."

"Just go straight through to my room, Crush.
There's tons of interesting stuff in there."

"Hi kid!"

"Would you like some tea and fairy cakes,
  Basher?" says Peter's mom.

"*Crusher*, Mom, and I don't think he would."

"Yes please," says Crusher.

"Come on, Claire, out you go. I'm sure
Crusher has better things to do.
Want to try my *Raiders of the Universe*
video, Crush?"

"OK, Pete. In a minute."

"Hey Crusher, you don't *have* to."

"I've got the whole set of *Captain Slaughter* comics to read in the tree house when you're ready, Crusher."

"Be right with you, Pete."

"If you don't want to come up in the tree house we can go and buy some candy at the store."

"Whatever you like, Pete. I'll just
finish up here."

"Three jawbreakers, please.
What are you having, Crusher?"

"What would your sister like?"

"Thanks for buying her the ice cream.
I'm sorry we've been stuck with her
all afternoon."

"Don't worry about it."

"We'll walk with Crusher to the corner, Mom."

"Thank you for the cakes and tea," says Crusher.

"It's a pleasure, Cruncher. Come again."